RESCUED ␣ᵢ THE DUKE OF BRIGHTON

DUKES, KISSES, AND BRIDAL WISHES

ELIZA HEATON

HIS
LOVE

CONTENTS

RESCUED BY THE DUKE OF BRIGHTON

    First printing, 2018
    Publisher
    His Everlasting Love Media
    info@hiseverlastinglove.com
    www.HisEverlastingLove.com

DEDICATED

to
my Grandma Jean.

*You dedicated your whole life to raising your children and your grand-
children, and we are all blessed because of the sacrifices that you
have made.*
*You rocked me to sleep when I was little and you met all of my needs
when I was sick. You brought me to church as a child, and whenever I
had a problem as an adult, you always prayed with me. I am eter-
nally grateful to you. I owe all of my successes in life to you.*

1

Miss Viola Endicott was failing at keeping the plentiful tears from sliding down her cheeks. She stood in the grand room of her family's manor in Brighton. She was trying so hard to be strong, but her tears told her that she was just not strong enough. Outside, it was dark, the kind of darkness that hid lurking omens. Distant thunder roiled in the black clouds, moving closer with each gust of the stiff winter wind. Thundersnow storms were rare in Brighton — another bad omen.

"Father, please do not go," she begged, her voice trembling. "We have just barely lost Mother. We cannot lose you too!" She brought her hands out of her crisp white apron covering her black mourning dress and pressed them together, her tiny porcelain hands folded in offered prayer.

The Viscount Endicott looked down at his eldest daughter, his withered face twisted into a look of sorrow and annoyance.

"My child," he implored, running a hand through thinning white hair. His wedding ring snagged a strand, just like it had

done many times before. His eyes filled with longing. Miss Endicott knew he no longer saw her, but rather was seeing her
mother in the way he looked at her. He softened visibly, and
clasped his soft, unworked hands around hers, kneeling down to
look her in the eye evenly. At seventeen, Miss Endicott knew she
looked most like her dear, departed mother. Though she had his
rounded nose, she had her mother's small, delicate chin and
wide heather grey eyes. She had her long oval face and black,
spirally hair that could never truly be tamed. It had been the
distant Irish blood in her that gave her such curls and such delicate skin.

"I am not going to die, my darling girl," he promised her, his
tone soft. He lifted his wiry gray eyebrows and stared implor-
ingly at her with ice blue eyes. "Our cousin the Earl of Surrey
needs my immediate help at our plantation in the Caribbean.
With my keen sense of finance and God's will, I can save us both
from bankruptcy and the shame of losing both property and
title. I am doing this for the good of everyone!"

Miss Endicott swallowed hard, taking in the heavy load of
information. It was not custom for men of the family to share
such news with their female counterparts and to do so implied a
great deal of trust. It was her job now to be worthy of it. Taking a
deep, steadying breath, she wiped away her tear, lifted her chin
and squared her shoulders. Her father was right. He was healthy,
and had no need to fear for his life.

"Stop being a ninny," she told herself. "This is not how
mother would have behaved and neither should you!"

"Tell me what to do father," she replied dutifully.

Lord Endicott smiled and patted his daughter lovingly on
the cheek.

"That is my girl," he praised her. "Now pay attention. Your
mother's brother, your Uncle Thomas, will be here to serve as

your guardian while I am to be away. You are to heed his word at all times, and you are to mind the new governesses as well."

"New Governesses?" Miss Endicott echoed, rising from her knees to watch as her father continued to give instructions to his butler, Roger. "What about Miss Tetherton and Ms. Seymore?"

Lord Endicott waved his hand in the air, losing his patience once more. "They are too old darling. Their teachings are out of date. Now be a good girl and heed me. Come and kiss me good-night and then be off to bed. I do not want you waking up the rest of your sisters."

Miss Endicott parted her lips to speak, but decided against it and bowed her head. Obediently she walked over to her father and gave him a kiss on his withered cheek.

"Very well father. Safe travels."

Miss Endicott left her father's chambers, the black morning dress weighing heavily on both her body and soul. Not only were the fabrics coarse and uncomfortable, but were moreso a constant reminder that she would never see her mother again. Once she realized there would be no reasoning with father, she immediately resigned her thoughts to taking off her ghastly dress and curling into the soft white blankets of her bed.

She was not ready for sleep but instead would hang a hooded lantern outside her window so she could watch the snow fall. She would count the snowflakes until dreams swept her away to happier times.

"Bessie," Miss Endicott greeted her chambermaid as she approached her room. "Be a dear and go fetch me some hot water with honey, would you? With just a sprig of tea?" The fourteen-year-old girl bobbed in a quick curtsey and scurried towards the servant stairs.

Viola liked Bessie. She was a good girl, but extremely timid. It often took her three times longer than normal to get ready for bed anytime Bessie was there to "assist" her. She knew she should be teaching the girl to move faster, but it was so much easier just to send her away to fetch a snack or a drink.

Inside her dressing chamber, Miss Endicott found her nightgown, and with quick fingers, began the unlacing of the tight corset. It was a dreadful task, but necessary, for sleeping in a corset could be extremely painful. By the time Bessie was back with her tea, she had changed into her nightgown, washed her face, and had brushed her unruly hair into a braid. Miss Endicott accepted the tea and sent the young girl off to bed. When the lantern was lit outside her window, and she was sure she was alone, Miss Endicott shuddered and let out a long sigh, before leaning back against the pillows.

Father was going. An uncle she barely knew was now her guardian. And her oldest and most beloved governesses were to be sent away first thing in the morning. Though Christmas was horrible with her mother's death, this was not by any means a good start to a new year either.

As she watched the snow fall steadily around the outside lantern, she found comfort in knowing that out of all the abrupt change, there would be at least one sure thing. Her best friend Charlie would be there for her.

MISS ENDICOTT OPENED her eyes to the sight of two gigantic blue eyes shielded by golden eyelashes staring at her from the side of her bed. Her youngest sister, Christina Marie, or Chrissy for short, had her chubby little hands planted on the duvet as she stared intently at Miss Endicott, waiting for her to wake up.

"Where is your nurse, Chrissy?" She asked, immediately sitting up. She reached down to the five-year-old, and she went willingly into her arms. Miss Endicott opened the covers and tucked her little sister in beside her. Bessie would be coming any moment with breakfast, and there would be no need to leave the bed just yet.

"Tell me now," she asked, stroking the little girl's hair. "Did you run away again?"

Chrissy did not speak. She never did. Instead, she just nodded. Even before their mother had gotten sick, Chrissy was never one to use words. Not that she needed them. Those bright blue eyes could speak volumes.

"Well you are going to feel dreadfully sorry for that in a moment," Miss Endicott scolded. "For we must say goodbye to your nurse this morning. And mine too. Father has hired new governesses, and we will not be seeing Miss Tetherton and Ms. Symore anymore."

The little girl made a pout with her cherub lips but gave no other reaction. Unlike most children, she did not cry out or make a fuss over most things. In her eyes shone an intelligence that went way beyond her years. Though she would never admit to anyone other than herself, Miss Endicott carried with the knowledge that Chrissy was her favorite of her sisters.

"Oy, what's this now mum?" Bessie asked, opening the bedroom doors wide so a servant could wheel in the breakfast tray.

"Where in God's teeth have you been, missy? Miss Thetherton has been all over the estate inside and out lookin' for you!"

"It is all right, Bessie," Viola said suddenly, putting up a slender hand to forestall complaints. "Chrissy and I will take breakfast in my bed this morning. Do be good and inform Miss Tetherton that Chrissy is safe and sound, would you?"

Bessie opened her mouth to insist otherwise but quickly

closed it. It would do no good to tell the Lady of the house what was and was not proper.

"Very well mum, very well. I'll go fetch her then and tell her all is right. But do please send Miss Christina Maria to her room afterward; she needs to be bathed and dressed before your uncle sees her."

Miss Endicott sat upright and tossed the covers off of her legs.

"My uncle? He is here already? I thought it would take him a week to get here!"

Bessie went about laying the porridge, toast, and sausage links out on the table along with the pot of strong black tea and a pitcher of fresh cream. As she set the table, she talked.

"Well Miss, according to your uncle's butler, he had received word from Lord Endicott just over a week ago, informing him of his need to leave and imploring him to come to take you ladies into his guardianship."

Father knew about this for a week and did not tell me? She felt a surge of disappointment but quickly beat it down. Now was not the time to feel sorry for herself.

"Well," Miss Endicott moved on, carrying Chrissy to the breakfast table. "What of the new governesses? Did you meet them?"

Miss Endicott watched as Bessie's smiling face twisted to one of chagrin.

"Well, yes mum."

"Are they nice? How do they seem?" Miss Endicott asked anxiously upon seeing Bessie's reaction.

Bessie averted her eyes, clearly not sure how to respond.

"Well...ye see mum. There's five of them."

"Yes, yes," Miss Endicott pushed getting agitated. "And?"

"And they seem lovely, mum. Real educated ladies. Except one."

"One is not educated?" Miss Endicott asked, confused.

"No mum, they all be educated you see. But the one, mum. The tall one. She's umm..."

"Well spit it out," Miss Endicott pushed, growing more agitated by the minute.

"Well, mum. She seems like a real fright of a lady."

2

Miss Endicott rifled through her closet, looking for her most grown-up gown. If she was to receive her uncle, she would not do so looking like a cowering girl done up in frilly pink bows. When she could not find anything, she ordered Bessie to go to her late mother's chambers to retrieve a dress.

"I want the sapphire blue one, with the square cut neckline," she explained.

"The silk?" Bessie asked, flustered. "But you'll freeze!"

"Nonsense," she replied, shooing Bessie away with a hand gesture. "I will wear my wool undergarments and my black gloves. Now go, I do not want to keep uncle waiting too long."

After breakfast, Miss Endicott had escorted Chrissy back to the care of Miss Tetherton and quickly checked on her three other sisters before hurrying back to her chambers to get dressed. Though the fires were burning brightly in every single hearth of the estate, there was still a chill within the walls.

Bessie came back with the gown, and she began to dress quickly. It was an autumn gown, with 3/4 length fitted sleeves with very little puff at the shoulders. Underneath the delicate satin was a double layer of muslin. Before she stepped into the dress, she pulled on her elbow-length black kidskin gloves so that from her fingertips to her shoulders would be covered.

Like her mother, Viola was a lean woman. Thankfully she was well-endowed, and the dress fit quite well despite the fact that her figure had not quite matured yet. If no one had ever seen the gown before, they would have thought it was made just for her. Bessie quickly finished her curls and applied just a touch of blush to her lady's cheeks. Viola slipped on the matching shoes and made her way towards her father's study where her uncle was waiting.

At the door, Miss Endicott paused, taking a steadying breath. She was not sure what manner of man her uncle had become; she just prayed that he was not an ill-tempered one. Bringing her knuckles to the door, she rapped once. A clear male voice yelled, "Enter!" from the other side.

Inside the room stood a tall dark-haired man stood by the fireplace. He was wearing black breeches, a white collared shirt, and a black vest. His black leather boots rose high to his knees. His silver embroidered ebony waistcoat was slung carelessly over the back of a cushioned chair facing the hearth. Like her mother and herself, he had dark gray eyes and a head of curly black locks. He had a stern chin and strong jawline, but when he looked up at her, his stiff bearing melted away, and he gave her a loving smile.

"My darling niece," he greeted her, beckoning her further into the room. "Come closer, so I can look at you."

Miss Endicott forced her feet to carry her forward, not quite sure what to expect. When she was close, he held out his hands and took her gloved fingers into his own.

"Look at you, my dear. You are the spitting image of Emmie.

Aside from your nose, I bet there is not a shred of your father in you, is there?"

"Well," Miss Endicott stammered, "Mother always said I had his head for numbers more than her head for directing housework."

Laughter boomed from Uncle Thomas, and he brought her close to kiss her cheeks.

"Very good girl, very good! I have no doubt a sense of humor will bring in a fine nobleman one day. Now come, sit with me and have some tea. We have much to discuss."

He waved her towards a table in the corner of the enormous and well decorated sitting room. It was a large and round, white marble thing held steady on dark oak legs. It was a vast enough table to sit eight people. Which was good because five women in plain somber dresses were already there, standing over their high-backed chairs, waiting for permission to be seated. *These*, Miss Endicott thought, *must be the new governesses.*

"Come ladies, do have a seat," Uncle Thomas instructed. He pulled out Miss Endicott's chair for her before taking his own.

"Viola," he began once everyone was seated. "With the parting of your blessed mother and your honorable father being called to business, I have been asked to take on the arduous task of looking after you and your sisters while he is away. Your father may have not mentioned this to you, but I am a rather busy man myself. While I may not have a title, I am the owner of the largest sheep farm and wool company this side of the Thames. I own several dye houses, lambing barns, fabric factories, and employ several hundred people.

"However," he added, his voice and chest swelling with pride. "When duty calls, duty calls. So here I am, bringing you the finest governesses that both your father and myself could buy."

Miss Endicott looked at him, aghast. "Uncle, are your telling me that you are not staying here with us?"

Thomas picked up her hand and patted it sympathetically. "I am afraid I am, my dear. Farming is a hard business, where the work is never done. I have farmhands and foremen, yes, but they could never do all that I do. But I promise you, I am leaving you in the very best of hands."

"But Uncle, I—"

"Young lady," a shrill voice rose up, interrupted her. "Have you not been taught your manners? Your uncle has spoken. It is not your duty to question, but to obey."

The high-pitched tone came from the tallest and thinnest of the women sitting across from her. She wore an out-of-date, high collared black dress made of simple calico and wool. Her hair, a dark brown, was piled high on her head in a large bun that threatened to tip over at any moment. Thin, pale lips drew a straight line above her chin and below a sharp, tiny nose. Her dark brown, nearly black eyes gave a startling resemblance to that of a mouse. Still, she was fairly young, certainly not older than thirty-five.

Uncle Thomas pulled his hand away to cough uncomfortably into it, looking from his niece to the head governess.

"She is right, Viola," he said, sounding almost uncertain. "May I introduce your head governess and your private tutor, Ms. Eleanor Broomsby. Going down the line from her left is Miss Talula Taverston, Ms. Lily Shadwell, Widow Galvinson, and Mrs. Katerina Brach. Her husband Claus is one of my new foremen just a few leagues away."

Viola and her sisters had always had English governesses, all of whom were considered old maids, and were no longer eligible to marry. Mrs. Katerina Brach, however, was both married and a foreigner, and Miss Endicott instantly felt the urge to befriend her.

"It is a pleasure to meet you all," Miss Endicott offered, nodding her head to each of them in turn.

"Well put," her uncle cheered, clapping his hands together. "Now, unfortunately, I must leave you to yourselves. Ms. Broomsby will be acting as your guardian while I am not here, but I can promise you that I will be back to check on things every nine days until your father returns. If an emergency should arise, Ms. Broomsby has an address she can send word to me."

Miss Endicott stood with her uncle, and he placed a chaste kiss on her cheek once more. "Be good my darling girl. If God is good, your father will be home within the year with a husband and new title for you."

"It is a wonder she is not married already," Ms. Broomsby spoke underneath her breath. Miss Endicott had heard the sneer in her voice. If her uncle heard it too, he gave no sign that he had. An uneasiness settled within Miss Endicott as if she knew there were about to be more difficult times ahead.

"Mind the governesses," her uncle said once more as he left the room. Once he was gone, a quietness settled over the library so cold that it could have frozen out the fire in the hearth.

Finally, to break the silence and the ice, Mrs. Brach cleared her throat and smiled.

"Vell now," she began, her German accent thick. "Shall ve meet the other little *frauleins?*"

3

"Heavens, V, she sounds ghastly," Charles Bringham III, the Duke of Brighton exclaimed quietly. He picked a honey biscuit off the doily on his plate and popped the entire thing into his mouth. "Thank God I do not have to put up with her."

The Duke of Brighton sat under the high ceiling of the drawing room. The warmth of the fireplace barely reaching him on the lavish sofa where he sat.

"You are not helping, Duke," Viola retorted wryly, slumping into her chair. It had been four weeks since her father had left for the sugar cane plantation, and her uncle had left for London. She had yet to receive post from Lord Endicott, but as promised, her uncle Thomas had come for a visit every nine days - even if it were sometimes only for a few hours. Since he had left, Miss Talula Taverston, Ms. Lily Shadwell, Widow Galvinson, and Mrs. Katerina Brach had all been exceptional governesses. They got along with their assigned children splendidly. Mrs. Brach especially had a knack for creating games when the girls were stuck indoors for days on end because of the heavy snow.

Ms. Broomsby, however, was a different story. She was wound as tight as a top despite her floppy excuse of a bun. Her version of teaching was to point out to Miss Endicott every little thing she did wrong, from how she comported herself in her lessons, to the fact that she preferred to dress and undress herself.

"A proper lady has no business undoing her own buttons!" she had said just that morning, her voice shrill. The old bat had no right to talk, however, seeing as that the only reason she even found out was because she had entered Miss Endicott's chambers without knocking, a very rude thing to do to a daughter of a Viscount.

Still, things were not too horrible. After all, Viola's childhood friend had just got back from serving as a Captain in the Queen's army, and despite having come back with a few bumps and bruises, he was still his easygoing, cheerful self. Though they had exchanged letters often, Miss Endicott had not realized how much she had missed her friend until he had shown up that early February morning.

"No? Not helping you say?" he answered, having the audacity to look innocently puzzled. "Perhaps not with my words, that is true," he admitted, rising and coming to stand before her. "But perhaps this trinket will help lift your spirits.

Viola straightened up immediately, a mischievous smile on her face.

"Why Charles! Did you bring me a gift?"

"Indeed I did," he told her, fishing his hand into his pocket. "I saw it in London a week ago, and I just thought, would Lady V not look just utterly perfect in it?"

He pulled out a purple velvet drawstring bag and presented it to Viola.

"Now that I am aware you have been experiencing troubles,"

he added more somberly, "I am doubly happy that I found it. I hope it lifts your spirits.

Viola's fingers trembled as she took the small velvet bag. It was only a couple years ago that the duke had started to call her "V" or "Lady V," and she immediately adored that she had her own nickname. This was her first gift from him, however, and a new type of excitement ran through her. Pulling the strings apart, she opened the bag and poured the contents into her hand.

She gasped when she saw the choker. It was cobalt blue, her favorite color. The wide, high quality blue ribbon was backed with a matching shade of velvet and had a black embroidered border. Dangling from it directly in the center was an ivory cameo, carved into a face that startlingly resembled her own. It was a beautiful gift, and not at all proper if it were to be given to just a childhood friend.

"Charles, I—"

"It looked so much like you, I could not pass it up," the duke informed her. Plucking it from her hands, he moved behind her chair so he could fasten it around her neck. As he brushed her curls away from her collarbone, she felt a hot shiver, a kind she had never felt before, slide up her spine.

"It must have cost you a fortune," she protested. "Would not this be a better present suited for a sweetheart or... or..."

"You," he finished for her, securing the choker in place. "It is suited for you," the duke said, and when she tried to turn to look at him, she beheld a smile she did not understand.

He moved around in front of her, seating himself on the settee across from her, that he had no difficulty in meeting her eyes evenly with his dark green ones. Viola felt a blush rise in her cheeks as she looked at him, that heated shiver making itself present again. *Has Charles always been this handsome?* As a child, his reddish-blonde hair and bulking figure gave him an odd form, and he often seemed out of place. But as a man, his bulkiness had been built into muscle, and that reddish blonde hair brought out the deep strength in eyes that grown mysteriously dark.

"V, look," he said, his tone serious. "There is something I want to talk to you about."

Before he could finish, the doors to the library were flung open, and there in all her fury, Ms. Broomsby came storming in.

"What is the meaning of this?" she demanded, her face red with rage. "I had to find out from your chambermaid that you were receiving male company? How dare you behave this way!" Ms. Broomsby reached down and grabbed Miss Endicott viciously by the arm, dragging her to her feet.

The duke stood up immediately, pulling Miss Endicott away from the enraged governess.

"How dare *you*, Madam?" he shot back, putting himself between Miss Endicott and the wretched woman.

"This is a daughter of Lord Endicott. You have no right to touch her as you would a common child. I demand you issue an apology immediately."

Ms. Broomsby's eyes all but glowed red with anger at the young man. Of course, he was right. If Viola reported her, she could lose her station. Yet on the other hand, she had clearly despised her the moment she had laid eyes upon her. You could see it on Ms. Broomsby's face, the questions of who Viola thought she was. As though she were flaunting her fine features and title? She had made the mistake from the start of thinking that Viola would be stupid and she could rule over her by wit, but Miss Endicott had taken delight in actually proving she could use her brain and pointed out often that she bored with her lessons because she understood them so quickly.

Ms. Broomsby forced a thin smile to spread across her lips, letting her shoulders ease slowly down from her ears.

"Your Grace, what I mean to say is," she replied, her voice becoming sugary sweet, "it is not at all proper for young ladies to receive gentlemen without a chaperone present. It is best you leave now, for Miss Endicott's reputation's sake, and return only when her uncle or Lord Endicott is present."

The duke and Viola knew that there was really no arguing the point, for it was a valid one. Under the rules of propriety, Miss Endicott was not to receive male callers without a guardian present, even if that certain caller had been her friend since she was seven years old. Giving in to society's rules, the duke bowed at his waist towards the governess.

"You are right," he admitted, his shoulders slumping a little in defeat, "I offer my apologies, Madam." Without waiting to hear a response, he turned his gaze and body to Viola, who's cheeks were stained with a blush of embarrassment. His look lingered, as though he had more to say, but did not dare. Picking up her hand delicately, the duke bowed in front of her to graze a kiss across her knuckles.

"It is always a pleasure to see you, my dear. Look for my letters, will you not?"

"Of course," Viola promised, wishing more than ever that she could just disappear into thin air, that she might be removed someplace far away from Ms. Broomsby. Without another word or even a glance towards the matron, the duke turned on his heel and walked proudly out of the library, not being at all delicate with the shutting of the heavy door.

4

The days after the duke left were an absolute horror. Ms. Broomsby grew stricter and angrier more and more each day. What was worse, her attitude was rubbing off on the other governesses. First, it started with Bridget's governess, Miss Taverston. Bridget was the second oldest daughter at the age of fifteen. She looked more like their father with her blonde hair and bright blue eyes.

What she lacked in understanding both numbers and geography, she gained back in embroidery and musical talents. Before, when her mother was alive and her governess was Miss Tetherton, the entire estate would be filled for hours on end with beautiful music from the pianoforte. Bridget loved to play and did so well that Miss Tetherton let her other lessons slide.

In the beginning of her employ, Miss Taverston had allowed her to continue that way. However, after being cornered and coerced by Ms. Broomsby, Miss Taverston started pulling Bridget away from her piano practice more and more often, until she was barely playing an hour a day.

Without her music, Bridget's upbeat and airy disposition

became more solemn and depressed. She was the first to start showing up in Viola's chambers after everyone was in bed for the night.

Elizabeth started showing up barely a week later, crawling into the large bed with Bridget and Viola for sisterly bonding. Elizabeth was the second youngest at seven years old. She was very much a hoyden, more like a boy than a girl. Despite her title and proper upbringing, she would constantly find ways to shear her golden curls up to her chin and had pleaded with her mother to let her wear breeches and shirts.

At the beginning of their relationship, Elizabeth's governess, Ms. Shadwell, had found the child odd but endearing. She was good with her lessons, as long as she was allowed to run about with the kitchen boys between afternoon tea and supper. Sadly, Broomsby got to Ms. Shadwell too. Whether it was by bullying or actual coercion, the old witch had begun changing the temperament of Ms. Shadwell, and she was soon spanking Elizabeth's bottom if she was caught running in the halls or wearing breeches.

As an act of rebellion, Elizabeth had taken her embroidery scissors to her hair and cut it so short that her hair barely curled over the top of her ears. When her governess had gone to awaken her the next morning, she screamed so loud the groundskeepers outside heard her. It took both Viola and Mrs. Brach to pull her away from the child.

"She is an ignorant little beast!" Ms. Broomsby had hissed in defense of Ms. Shadwell's actions. "She will never be a lady!"

Elizabeth was quick to shoot back, "Well if you are what a lady is, then I never want to be one!"

Since that time, whether the governesses liked it or not, Viola had demanded that she and Elizabeth receive their lessons in the same room, so that she could keep an eye on Ms. Shadwell. Margaret, who was eleven, and Chrissy, however, were having no problems with their governesses or their lessons yet, and Viola prayed nightly that it would continue to be so until she could speak to her father about the violent behavior Ms. Broomsby was spreading to the other governesses.

"ZEY ARE NOT BAD CHILDREN," Mrs. Brach countered in her thick German accent. She picked up the teapot from the table and poured herself and Widow Galveson each a cup of tea. "I do not understand vy Eleanor hates zem so!"

Nearly three months had gone by since they had arrived at their new governing post and much had changed. Eleanor had always been a bitter presence, but in the beginning, Lily and Talula had seemed like patient, well-educated ladies. Now their tempers were short, and their manner of teaching had grown strict and spiteful.

"I do not understand it either," Widow Galveson agreed. "She has a way of turning people into their worst selves!" It was a bold statement, but a true one. The widow had experienced herself Eleanor's twisting and bullying behavior. More than once the woman had cornered her and attempted to whisper falsities in her ear about her charge, young Margaret. And she was such a sweet girl!

Margaret loved to sing and dance and poured herself over her literature books. Embroidery and sewing were not her strong suits, but she would be a lady of leisure anyway.

Ms. Broomsby had attempted to report that the girl was being secretly disrespectful, rattling off offenses such as putting salt in the sugar bowl and getting one of her chambermaids to complete her embroidery work for her. These were silly, and in Widow Galveson's opinion, tacky rumors.

Still, she knew that Eleanor was not to be messed with. She

had an ill feeling about her, and everyone knew it. The staff stayed away from her as much as possible, and she was even able to convince the girls' uncle Thomas to refuse a meeting with Lady Endicott on his last two visits to the estate. Eleanor was a growing concern, and she often pondered on whether or not the woman was above causing bodily harm to those who would not listen to her.

"The children are becoming so frightened that they all have started sleeping in Viola's chambers. They do not know I know, but I caught Elizabeth going into her eldest sister's room just after the stroke of ten – a whole hour after the girl was supposed to be in bed."

Mrs. Brach shook her head and clucked her tongue at the news. Of course, she knew her little Chrissy did the same but had known that her habit went back long before the governesses ever arrived. The young girl reminded her of the faery folk, and she enjoyed her quiet nature. It seemed almost natural that she should be able to appear and disappear at her own will.

Before she could speak her thoughts, the door to Widow Galveson's room opened, and the devil herself stepped in.

"It is incredibly impolite to enter someone's personal quarters without at least knocking first," Widow Galveson said loudly, not even bothering to look up at the woman. "You will do well to close the door and do so."

Ms. Broomsby scowled and stood her ground. "I'll do no such thing. You are a guest in this house, and Sir Thomas has left me in charge while he is away. I have the right to enter any room I so choose, as long as I have a key to it." She ended with an indignant huff and strolled further into the room.

"Besides," she added, changing her tone to a sweeter note. "I'm here in your best interest. I have news of an ill-behaved charge."

5

M iss Endicott read the words of the duke's letter over and over again, certain phrases standing out more than others.

MY DARLING V...I miss your smile...I worry for your house...No child of nobility should be treated such a way...

IN THE TEN years of their friendship, he had never called her darling in a letter. True he had mentioned missing her smile, but it was while he was away in India or Africa while on business for the Queen. Besides, it seemed so innocent for him to say it then. Now things felt different between them, more serious. The idea of him genuinely missing her smile gave her her first burst of happiness she had felt in some time.

After glancing over her shoulder to make sure her sisters were fast asleep, she began to word her reply.

DEAR DUKE,

I MUST ADMIT *that I miss you too. Circumstances here have brought our already depressed mood even farther down. I am trying to be brave and strong for the little ones, but it seems everywhere I turn Broomsby is there, lurking like an angel of death. However, your letter gives me strength. I must somehow find a way around the witch so that I can see my uncle when he next comes to visit.*

We finally received a letter from Father last week. Things in the Caribbean are straightening themselves out painfully slow. It appears our cousin has caused our family a great deal of trouble by his misuse of fiduciary knowledge. I fear that it will be at least another year before we see him again.

Your kind words warm my heart. In your letter to talk of matters of the future needing to be discussed. What, pray tell, could these matters be?

MISS ENDICOTT SMILED as she wrote the letter. She had a feeling that those matters of the future included a marriage proposal from the duke. The very idea filled her heart with warmth and excitement. Her father had always approved of Charles since he had been childhood friends with the old duke before his death. Mother had always hinted at a marriage, but never let on which son would marry which daughter. On top of a noble title, the old duke and his sons also had a sizable stake in the sugar cane plantation in the Caribbean, which Charles was now in charge of.

Under dying candlelight, she finished writing out her letter before signing it with the phrase

With Great Affection,
Lady V

AFTER SHE FINISHED WRITING her letter and had sealed it, Miss Endicott still could not get her mind to rest. There were so many things bothering her that sleep rarely visited her anymore. Not to mention she now four pairs of tiny feet constantly kicking and tugging at her covers.

Going to the window, she took in the beauty of the night. The moon was not even halfway full, but it was bright and illuminated the east facing gardens. Spring was just around the corner. The snow was all but gone, and young buds of daffodils and Easter lilies were breaking through the thawing earth.

She missed her mother. Before she had gotten sick, her mother would always take nightly strolls in the garden with her father. Miss Endicott would watch them through her window as they walked hand in hand. Not many nobles were able to marry for love, but ever since she was a little girl she had always seen and felt the high feelings between her parents.

Her thoughts drifted once more to Charles, and for a moment she thought of what a marriage with him would be like. He would use kind words, of that she was sure. Perhaps he would touch her with his soft hands. Not only was he attractive, but he was a man who enjoyed a good sense of humor and preferred to let his money talk for him if anyone ever showed judgment about him not having a title. Marrying him, she decided, would make her extremely happy.

Miss Endicott was remembering the endearing words that Charles had written her when she suddenly had an idea. As far as she knew, Broomsby had not been intercepting their post. If she had, Miss Endicott was quite certain she would have taken Charles's letters by now. A plan was beginning to form in her head as she returned to her writing desk. If she could not get around the governess while her uncle visited, maybe she could convince her that she was supposed to go London to visit him.

UNTITLED

~

Miss Endicott began to set her plan in motion first thing in the morning. First, she slipped out of house to make sure that she could hand the letter to the postmaster himself. She slipped the letter she had penned in her uncle's handwriting in with the rest of the letters and delivered them to the kitchen where they would be dispersed. Next, she set about creating tasks that would be arduous for Broomsby to complete each day. If she was going to act like the Matron of the house, then she would have to deal with the hardships of being one.

Normally Miss Endicott was not a trickster. She enjoyed being a lady, and unlike some other girls of her age and status, she did not feel the need to be wicked. However desperate times had called for desperate measures. The first trick she decided to play was with Broomsby's tooth powder. While she was having lunch, Viola snuck into her room, emptied the contents of the tin, and replaced it with flour. After that, she pulled back the sheet on her bed and sprinkled a dozen or so tiny beetles she had dug up from the nearest garden over the blanket. They were not poisonous, but if bitten by them, a person would begin to itch incessantly. If bitten more than two or three times, a mild fever would set in. Lastly, she poured honey into her enemy's hair soap. With luck, the tricks would be enough to keep Broomsby occupied until her trip to London. By the end of the day, she knew that the first part of her plan had worked when she and her sisters were called into her father's study before bedtime.

"Your Uncle has called me away to London to discuss important business concerning you girls," she said sharply. "While I am away, Ms. Shadwell will be left in charge. She is to report everything to me as it happens, so do not try any foolishness. Am I understood?" She looked at each in turn. No one dared utter so much as a word. "Good. Now, I must leave in two days' time, and until then I am still in charge!" She smirked at the girls.

She feels like she has total control over us. Miss Endicott struggled to combat the urge to smile, thinking how completely untrue this was. In fact, she felt like her plan might actually work. Hope sprung in her chest as she let her thoughts drift being free of the wretched woman. *Once she is gone,* Miss Endicott thought to herself as Broomsby barked on, *I will tell uncle Thomas everything that has happened. Every single detail of her cruelty. Then I will implore him to meet with Charles, that we might live happily ever after.*

6

The next few days were filled with a whirlwind of activity. Just as she hoped, Viola's little tricks went off splendidly. The very next morning Broomsby woke up covered in bug bites and was itching like crazy. She had red splotches all over hands and face, even a big one right on the tip of her nose. Then, when she tried to take a cool bath to lower the swelling and redness, she found that after washing her hair it was untamable. Large knots caught the strands of hair in strange configurations that try as she might, she could not get combed out.

With her being so distracted, Miss Endicott's plan was beginning to work. After just a few hours of not being under her thumb, the other governesses were finally getting some breathing room. As the day wore on, they found themselves laughing and enjoying their charges once again. It was as if the world had started to right itself once again.

Since Broomsby was confined to her room all day, Miss Endicott had the chance to practice what she would try to say to her uncle. She had to find a way to report all of the terrible things the governess was doing and saying without sounding like a child. Finally, she decided to confide in Mrs. Brach regarding her plan.

"Ha!" The German governess laughed, slapping her knee. "Zat is *wunderbar!* Very clever, child. What do you need my help with?"

Viola breathed a sigh of relief when she realized she had the immediate support of the woman. "I need someone to stand with me when my uncle gets here to explain all the horrid things Broomsby has been getting away with. My sisters are too young to ask to do it, and I fear he will think we are just spoiled children. But if I have a governess willing to stand with me, I believe he will take my complaints more seriously."

"Absolutely, I vill do this," Mrs. Brach promised. "Today without her has been *wunderbar*. It would be best that she leave this place as soon as possible."

Miss Endicott was beyond thrilled that her plan was going so well. All she had to do now was make sure that no matter what, Broomsby was in the carriage first thing tomorrow morning for London. Just as she was getting ready to go check on the carriage, however, she heard the one sound that could ruin everything.

The trumpets that announced company was at the gate blared loudly through the estate, sending Miss Endicott's heart into overdrive. Other than her Uncle and Charles, they had received no guests since her father had left. She knew it was not Charles for his last letter was posted from Paris, and he had written that he would be there for several more weeks on business for his father. It could only mean one thing; that her uncle had come to visit early.

Gathering up her skirts, Miss Endicott ran as fast as she could out to the courtyard. It was highly unladylike for a woman of her stature to run, but the situation was indeed dire. She *had* to get to her uncle Thomas before Broomsby did.

Thomas's eyebrows shot up in surprise when he saw his eldest niece running towards him at full speed. Descending from his horse, he landed on his feet just in time to grasp her shoulders to stop her from plowing straight into him.

"Viola! What is the meaning of this? What is the matter? Where did you come from? Where is Ms. Broomsby?"

"Uncle, please," she implored, tugging at his hand and ignoring his barrage of questions. "You must come with me right away. Mrs. Brach and I must speak with you privately."

"Whatever for?" Thomas asked, walking in the direction Viola was leading him. "This is most odd. Where is Ms. Broomsby? Is she sick?"

"No. Well, yes. But that is not why I— you see it is imperative that I speak with you alone Uncle. Ms. Broomsby has been—"

Her Uncle Thomas stopped in his tracks, his concentration turned fully towards the disgruntled figure at the top of the granite staircase. "God's teeth, madam. What on Earth happened to you?"

Ms. Broomsby hovered at the top of the stairs, looking like the witch that she was. Her long black dress was speckled with white dust. Her hair, bedraggled and knotted, stuck out in odd shapes all over her head. The fever from the beetle bites had left her face flushed, with those bright red splotches from the bites glowing even redder than the fever rash. Her lips were white and chapped from flaked flour and spittle, and her left eyelid must have received several bites for it could not open all the way.

"Your niece happened to me, that's what!" Ms. Broomsby shot back, her voice shrill as she pointed an accusing finger at Viola. "She put beetles in my bed, I know it was her! And someone put flour in my tooth powder and sap in my hair soap! She is an evil little thing, I tell you!

Uncle Thomas looked down at his niece in bewilderment. He did not know her well, but from the little time they had spent together, Viola could see that he thought it hardly like her.

"Is this true?" he asked, his tone serious.

Miss Endicott bit her lip. She was caught, true, but if she could just get him to speak with Mrs. Brach then maybe she still had a chance to right things.

"Well, yes, but Uncle I desperately needed to talk to you, and it was the only way I could distract her enough to—"

"Enough," Thomas said, his tone laced with anger. "You are a woman of seventeen, Viola, and this type of behavior is beneath you. Why, your mother would be rolling over in her grave right now if she could see what you have done!"

"Uncle you do not understand, I—" Viola felt tears rising in her throat as she tried to push the words she needed to say out of her. Everything was going wrong so fast!

"Go to your chambers, young lady," Thomas commanded. His voice did not have an ounce of give to it. "I will deal with you later."

Without another word, he released himself from her embrace and strode up the steps towards the disheveled governess.

"Come, Madam," he said, holding out his arm to her. "We clearly have much to discuss."

Miss Endicott felt her heart drop to her feet as her Uncle disappeared up the steps into the house with Ms. Broomsby. Her plan had failed, and now things were going to be even worse than before.

Two Weeks Later

MISS ENDICOTT HELD the letter in her trembling fingertips, reading the words over and over again. If it were any other circumstance, this letter would be an indication that she was about to experience the greatest happiness possible in life. Charles, sweet, caring Charles, had asked her in a letter to wait for him. It was not quite a marriage proposal, but it was proof that Charles loved her, and wanted her for more than just a friend.

The choker he had gifted to her felt heavy around her neck, making her ever more aware of his absence. She missed his hugs, his gentle teasing. She missed hearing him call her *Lady V* in person. In the letter the words *I have plans to meet with your father* kept standing out on the page. A letter from the Viscount had arrived just last week from the sugar cane plantation in the Caribbean, informing them all that it would be two more years until he would be able to come home due to some 'spectacularly sound' investment opportunities.

Two years. She could not ask Charles to wait that long! How could he? A man in his prime with such wealth, a handsome face and vigorous spirit was bound to draw the adoring attention from every noble lady from all across the continent.

Since her plan to oust Ms. Broomsby was ousted weeks ago, she had been confined to her rooms. She ate, slept, bathed, and had her lessons in the three compartments that were hers. It was amazing how quickly once large spaces could seem so small when one was never allowed to leave them. She was allowed to receive no guests save for Bessie and Ms. Broomsby, who had recovered quickly from the tricks she had played upon her. Her only reprieve was that once every two or three days Mrs. Brach or Widow Galveson had managed to sneak her younger sisters into her chambers in the middle of the night so that they could visit.

However, earlier that night the Widow Galveson had come to inform her that they had been found out and that the visits were no longer safe to make. According to Widow Galveson's recount, Broomsby had become extremely cruel, if not abusive to her younger sisters when she found that they were being snuck in to see their eldest sister. Not wanting to risk their safety, Viola made the Widow swear she would no longer encourage the other children to see her. As for Mrs. Brach, the moment Broomsby found out she was ready to aid Miss Endicott in her scheme, she had both her and her husband removed from the grounds immediately.

Out of fear of the vindictive Ms. Broomsby, Miss Endicott had lost any companion she might have had at her home estate. Feeling lonelier than ever, she picked up her quill and began to write. Tears rolled down her cheeks as she implored Charles to forget about her and their plans to be together. Her dreams of living a happy and stress free life with Charles fell apart, for she knew that no man, no matter how patient, would wait three years in the prime of his life for a bride.

7

C harles read over the letter he had just received from one of the cabin boys. It had been lost, then redirected, then lost and redirected again many times before it made it to him almost three months after Miss Endicott had sent it to him. It had been folded and crumpled many times by many handlers. But even so, the moment he opened it, he knew that the running of the ink was not from wear and tear, but from Viola's tears.

In the letter she made the bold confession of loving him, making his heart nearly burst out of his chest with joy. But the happiness was short-lived, for as the letter wore on, he found that she was imploring him to leave her behind. She had lost all hope, and would be forced to wait until her father came back to regain so much as a speck of it.

Little did she know, that the moment Charles had sent his last letter to her, he had boarded the next ship setting sale for the Americas. The ship had docked in Barbados for a few weeks to load up on supplies and fresh water when the cabin boy had picked up the bundle of letters at the town's only general store/post office. In two weeks' time, he would be in Jamaica, where he would find the Viscount's sugar cane plantation, and where he would be asking for Viola's hand in marriage.

Anger seethed through him as he pictured the wretched governess laying her hands on any of the Viscount's daughters. He was in love with Viola, yes, but he adored them all. They were good girls, all of them, and deserved better in life than this. The moment he read the letter he began to form a new plan. He would not just be taking Viola away from such a situation. He would find a way to take all of the Viscount's daughters away.

LORD ENDICOTT ROSE to his feet as he saw a familiar face appear at the door of his study. His bushy white eyebrows rose high as a wide smile spread across his face. There in front of him stood the Duke of Brighton. Other than his cousin, who had dimwittedly almost cost the plantation a fortune due to the overpayment for perishable goods that went bad, the Viscount had not seen a familiar face since he had left his home nearly a year ago.

Seeing the young man again gave him about of homesickness so strong he struggled with the knot in his throat that threatened to choke him with tears. Clearing his throat, he came around his large oak desk and grasped the duke's hand in a strong handshake.

"Good to see you, Duke," he said jovially. "Right good to see you. Are you here to check on your investments? I assure you they are doing much better since I have arrived." He added the last remark with a chuckle and waved his guest toward one the brown leather high-backed chairs in front of his desk.

"Care for a brandy? No, wait. You are in the Caribbean; you will want rum." The Viscount nodded to the servant standing in the corner. The man immediately busied himself with preparing two tumblers of white Caribbean rum for the gentlemen, and then in pouring two glasses of fresh water as it was not customary to drink the rich beverage without a water back.

Charles smiled at the old Viscount, feeling a familial affection for him. Like his own father had experienced, the years and stress of being a nobleman were starting to wear on the Viscount's face. Wrinkles were deeper, stomachs were rounder, and comically, sideburns had become more wiry, replacing smooth jet black hair with white whiskers.

He took the seat that was offered and unbuttoned his waistcoat. The humidity of the island was overwhelming in the room, even with the windows open.

"Yes," he answered, accepting the rum before reclining into the chair. "I did indeed come down here to check on my investments."

"I knew it!" the Viscount replied, sounding triumphant.

"However, I have come to discuss something else with you. Something much more dire."

The Viscount studied the young duke's face. There was not a hint of humor in his eyes as though he suspected his guest brought news that would be unpleasant to hear. The duke set his jaw, feeling his face grow rigid even as he felt his shoulders begin to slump from the enormous stress weighing him down. He felt older than his two and twenty years, as though this trip had suddenly aged him.

"Something has happened with the children," the Viscount said. It was not a question. He knew that the duke had always been sweet on his Viola since they were children. The duke knew it was the Viscount's hope to have them married someday.

Charles nodded his head solemnly. Taking a deep breath, the Viscount swallowed the contents of his tumbler before sitting it down on his desk with a loud thunk. "All right then young man. Tell me everything, and do not spare any of the details. What has happened to my children?

8

SIX WEEKS LATER

Anger swept through Miss Endicott as she passed back and forth in her room. Occasionally, she would glance over to her bed where little Chrissy lay sleeping among the pillows. Across her cherub face were five red marks that clearly showed the shape of fingers. Though her tears had stopped, the tracks of them left little white lines going across her innocent face. When Widow Galveson had first brought Chrissy to her room, she was angry at her for risking Chrissy's safety. Then she heard the sniffles and looked closer at her baby sister.

"Tell me what happened," she demanded, scooping her the little girl up into her arms as she ushered the Widow inside.

"The others have gotten worse," the governess had said fearfully. "They've turned cruel just like Ms. Broomsby. You must do something about her, my Lady. She is not stable!"

"Tell me what happened to Chrissy," Viola repeated through gritted teeth.

The Widow Galveson proceeded to go into the tale of how the Broomsby and the other two governesses had gathered the children into the library for a group lesson. They were to have a spelling bee to see who had been doing a better job as a governess.

"The girls knew it wasn't about their education," the widow said, shaking her head. "They knew, and they didn't want to play. That was when that old witch started threatening them. First, it was going to be without supper, but when they still said no she threatened to beat them. Well, Elizabeth, Margaret, and Bridget all gave in and began the game. But when it was little Chrissy's turn...well, she just wouldn't do it."

She had raised her shoulders up and down in a shrug as if she had been hopeless in doing anything else but that. The woman had aged considerably since she had arrived at the estate, but then again, they all had. Over the last year, birthdays and holidays had stopped being celebrated. The house had gone cold and quiet, leaving nothing for those living inside of it to do aside from growing older and more somber.

"Chrissy is always a quiet girl," she had continued. "Even when Mrs. Brach was here, she never spoke much. But she's an intelligent girl and has beautiful penmanship. It's always been easy to see that though quiet, she was very bright." Her chin had begun to tremble, and her eyes had welled up with tears. As Miss Endicott watched the older woman fall apart, she felt her heart being ripped in two. She knew what she was about to hear next, but that did not make it any easier to listen to.

"When Chrissy wouldn't play into her game, Broomsby started getting upset. She called her horrible, vile names. Names that should never be used in discussing a six-year-old child! And then...then she did it. When she realized that she wasn't going to win, she just reached her hand back as far as it would go, and slapped little Chrissy so hard across the face we could hear her teeth rattle!"

Widow Galveson did not stay long after the telling the tale, but when she tried to take Chrissy with her, Viola refused. She was never letting the child out of her sight again. She had snuggled and sang to Chrissy until she had fallen asleep. Only when her sister was resting peacefully did Viola begin pacing the floor. She was going over her options in her head when the trumpet from the gate sounded so suddenly she nearly jumped out of her skin.

Looking out her window, she saw that it was already dark. *Who in the world is visiting at this hour?* Moments later, Bessie came bursting through her door in great excitement with her pale cheeks flushed and her eyes bright. Her smile was so wide it threatened to pop right off of her face.

"What is it, Bessie? Is it uncle Thomas? Will he finally talk to me?" Viola asked, growing excited as well.

"No my lady!" Bessie exclaimed, holding up Viola's dressing robe for her. "It's the Viscount, he's back! And the duke is with him!"

Happiness and shock tore through Miss Endicott as she quickly put the dressing robe on. Her fingers trembled as she tied the sash around her waist and slipped her feet into her slippers. Was Broomsby's tyranny really about to end? As soon as her slippers were on her feet, she tore out of the room, moving as quickly as she could towards the steps that led down to the foyer. As she reached the top of them, she saw her father's white hair and the duke's reddish blond locks and began to sob.

"Father! Father I cannot believe it, you are home!" The tears came thick and fast as she made her way down the steps as fast as she could.

The Viscount opened his arms as Viola made it to the last step, and swept her up into a tight hug. She knew she looked tired and too thin. She felt the outrage spark through him.

CHARLES HAD SHARED the letters Viola had written to him about the governess's maltreatment, but nothing had prepared him for how his daughter looked. She barely looked like a lady of good breeding anymore, with her sallow cheeks and the dark circles under her eyes.

"Where is she?" he growled, when he could finally let go of his daughter.

From the left, the familiar shrill voice of Ms. Broomsby filled the room. She walked tall and proud toward the father and daughter, her chin held high.

"Ah, Lord Endicott. Welcome home. I am Ms. Eleanor Broomsby. I am your daughter's governess and have been taking care of your children while you have been away." She said it with such pride that he wondered if the woman was insane. Had she really thought that the sudden visit would be a call to praise her efforts?"

"Guards!" the Viscount called, his eyes staring coldly at the woman. Immediately ten guards came in through the main doors. "Arrest this woman!"

Broomsby's eyes went big and bright as the color drained out of her face. "What is the meaning of this?" she yelled, backing away.

"Find the other two as well," the Viscount commanded, feeling the fury coursing through his veins, "Lily Shadwell and Talula Talverson."

TWO OF THE guards pulled a screaming Ms. Broomsby out the door as the others went through the house to find the other two cruel governesses. As they did so, the rest of the house began to stir, and soon all of Viola's sisters came tumbling down the stairs to hug their father. Letting the little ones have their father for a few moments, Viola allowed Charles to pull her to the side.

"How is this happening?" she asked. Tears were still rolling down her cheeks, but she did not care. They were no longer tears of sorrow, but rather of happiness. "What did you do?"

Charles recounted his journey to the Caribbean after receiving her second letter. He told her of how disappointed he was in the lack of care her Uncle had provided, so he had convinced his father to book passage for him so he could go down to check on the sugar cane plantation.

"I had planned on talking to your father anyway, but after I received your last letter I knew I had to convince him to come back with me."

VIOLA STARED out over the ocean, watching the bright morning sun lift its way out of the mass of blue water. The air was warm and smelled of salt as it slipped over her face. Below her, the gardens of exotic flowers had come into full bloom and were looking up at her in bright colors of gold and orange, purple and blue, brilliant green and blinding yellow. Right outside the stone gate was their beach, with soft, white sand and little waves of blue and white foam from the ocean washing up tiny crabs and seashells. *It is paradise here*, she thought.

"How are you feeling this morning, my darling Duchess of Brighton?"

Viola blushed as Charles brushed a loving kiss across her cheek. It had been nearly six months since he and her father had come to rescue them. After Broomsby and the other two governesses had been arrested and taken away, the Viscount announced his plans to bring his children with him back to the sugar cane plantation where, to Viola and the duke's delight, the young couple would be married.

With the warmth of the Caribbean and the year of cruelty

behind them, the young ladies had thrown out their mourning gowns with glee, replacing them with cotton fabrics dyed in soft yellows, purples, and pinks. The only dark color Viola wore anymore, was the lapis blue choker that Charles had given her that long ago day. It had become a symbol of solace to her, especially in the months where she had lost all hope.

Gone were the days of staying indoors and having strict mealtimes. They danced their bare feet in the sand near the ocean, they flew kites in the warm wind and indulged in the Caribbean delicacies such as fried plantains and conch fritters. They were finally happy once again.

"Wonderful," she replied finally. She turned away from the balcony and joined Charles at the breakfast table. Before she could take her chair, he wrapped his arms around her waist and pulled her into his lap. She giggled as he did so, not able to believe how happy she was feeling.

"Really?" he asked, teasing her. "Wonderful, eh?"

Laughing, she leaned down to her husband to kiss his lips. "Not just wonderful," she told him. "Perfect."

FREE EBOOK

Receive a FREE inspirational Regency Ebook by visiting our website and signing up for our emailing list.
Click the link to enter www.HisEverLastingLove.com in your web browser.

The newsletter will also provide information on upcoming new books and new music.

THANK YOU!

Thank you so much for reading our book. We hope you enjoyed it.

If you liked this book, we would really appreciate a five-star review on Amazon or Goodreads. Every review you take the time to write makes an enormous impact on our writers' lives. Reviews really encourage our authors and let them know the positive things you enjoyed about their creativity.

Thank you again! I hope this book brightened your day.

ABOUT THE AUTHOR

Eliza Heaton grew up enjoying the amazing landscapes of her hometown in Perth, near Edinburgh, Scotland. She often visited the Isle of Skye with her parents during her summers as a child and dreamed of becoming a writer. She attended university in Edinburgh where she completed her Masters in English Literature with a focus on the Victorian and Regency periods.

Eliza currently lives in the Dean Village area of Edinburgh, Scotland, where she can walk along the Water of Leith creating the characters for her books. Cathedrals, statues of viscounts, and castles welcome her as she walks and imagines the perfect love story to write next.